Prehistoric Creatures

Dinosaur Spikes and Necks

Joanne Mattern
Reading consultant: Susan Nations, M.Ed., author/literacy coach/consultant

WR WEEKLY READER
EARLY LEARNING LIBRARY

Please visit our web site at: **www.earlyliteracy.cc**
For a free color catalog describing Weekly Reader® Early Learning Library's
list of high-quality books, call 1-877-445-5824 (USA) or 1-800-387-3178 (Canada).
Weekly Reader® Early Learning Library's fax: (414) 336-0164.

Library of Congress Cataloging-in-Publication Data

Mattern, Joanne, 1963-
    Dinosaur spikes and necks / Joanne Mattern.
      p. cm. — (Prehistoric creatures)
    Includes bibliographical references and index.
    ISBN 0-8368-4898-5 (lib. bdg.)
    ISBN 0-8368-4905-1 (softcover)
    1. Dinosaur—Juvenile literature. I. Title. II. Series.
QE861.5.M347   2005
  567.9—dc22   2005042871

This edition first published in 2006 by
Weekly Reader® Early Learning Library
A Member of the WRC Media Family of Companies
330 West Olive Street, Suite 100
Milwaukee, WI 53212 USA

Managing editor: Valerie J. Weber
Art direction and design: Tammy West

Illustrations: John Alston, Lisa Alderson, Dougal Dixon, Simon Mendez, Luis Rey

Printed in the United States of America

1 2 3 4 5 6 7 8 9 09 08 07 06 05

Long before there were people there were dinosaurs and other prehistoric creatures.

They roamed lands around the world. These creatures came in many shapes and sizes. Some had claws or sharp teeth. Others had spikes, long tails, or wings.

In this book, you will read about spikes and necks. Look for a label with the creature's name. You will also see how to say its name.

Stegosaurus
(STEG-oh-SAWR-us)

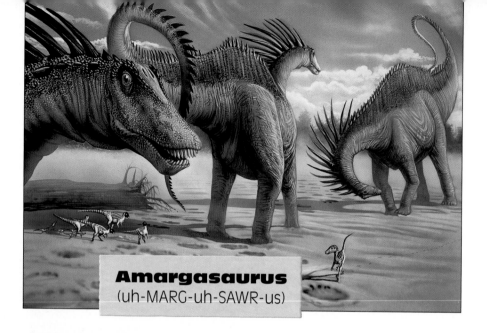

Amargasaurus
(uh-MARG-uh-SAWR-us)

Spiky Dinosaurs

Spikes helped dinosaurs protect themselves from
predators who wanted to eat them. Predators
would not like to chomp down on spikes! Spikes
could also be used as weapons in a fight against
another dinosaur.

    These dinosaurs had lots of spikes! Two rows of
spikes ran down their backs. A row of sharp spikes
stuck out on their tails, too.

Horned Head

Dinosaurs had many other ways to protect themselves. This dinosaur may have used its heavy head to hit other animals. A horn grew on its nose, and two more horns stuck out above its eyes. These horns were too light to use against other animals.

Ceratosaurus
(ser-RAT-uh-SAWR-us)

Stegosaurus Spikes

These dinosaurs had spikes and **plates** on their backs and tails. Plates are large, flat pieces of bone that stick out from an animal's body. When one of these dinosaurs swung its tail, the spikes on the end made a scary weapon!

Spikes? Yikes!

This dinosaur was clothed in **armor**. Armor is a tough covering that protects an animal's body. Thick, bumpy skin covered this creature's back and tail. Long, sharp spikes stuck out of its neck and shoulders. These spikes protected the dinosaur's head. A predator would get a nasty mouthful if it bit this creature!

Sauropelta
(SAWR-oh-PEL-tah)

7

Struthiosaurus
(STROO-thee-oh-SAWR-us)

Little Spiker

This dinosaur's body was about the size of a large dog's.
Spikes grew down its tail and back. Two longer spikes
stuck out of its shoulders. These spikes made it hard
for other animals to attack this creature.

Spiked Heads

The dinosaurs in this group all had spikes on their heads. Some spikes were small. Those spikes protected the dinosaurs. They were good weapons in a fight. Big horns grew above some of these dinosaurs' snouts.

Ceratopsians
(SER-uh-TOP-see-ins)

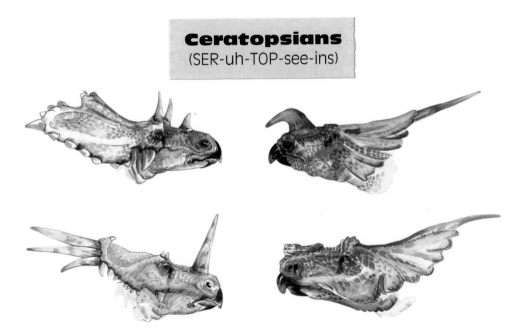

Three-Horned Face

This dinosaur's name means "three-horned face."
This creature weighed almost as much as an
elephant! Two long spikes rose above its eyes. The
third spike was shorter and stood on the dinosaur's
snout. Like those on other dinosaurs, this creature's
spikes helped the dinosaur protect itself.

Triceratops
(try-SER-uh-tops)

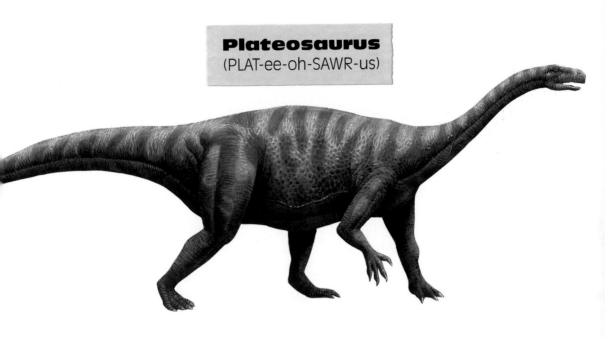

Plateosaurus
(PLAT-ee-oh-SAWR-us)

Long Necks

Necks are an important part of a dinosaur's body, too. The neck holds up the head. A dinosaur's neck could even help it find food!

These dinosaurs ate leaves. Their long necks helped them reach high into the trees to get their food.

Eating High and Low

This dinosaur also stretched its neck to munch on tree leaves. It could also bend low to eat grass. It swung its neck in a big arc to help it look for food.

Diplodocus
(dih-PLOD-uh-kus)

Neck Bones

Dinosaur bones help scientists learn what the dinosaurs looked like. In 1999, scientists found four neck bones from this dinosaur. The bones were very big. Their size helped scientists figure out how long the dinosaur's neck was.

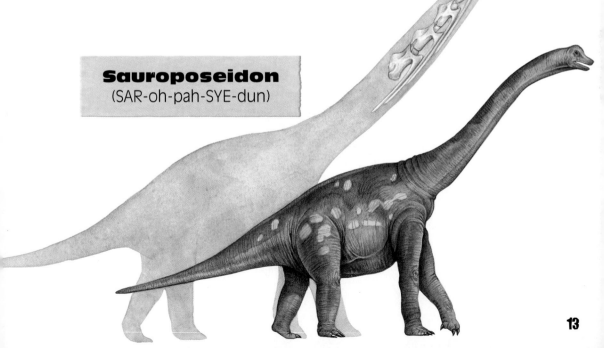

Sauroposeidon
(SAR-oh-pah-SYE-dun)

As Big as a Building!

This dinosaur was the longest in the world. Scientists think it may have been bigger than a three-story building laid on its side! Its neck and tail were the longest parts of its body. So far, scientists have found only one skeleton of this dinosaur.

Seismosaurus
(SIZE-moh-SAWR-us)

Big Dinosaur,
Light Neck Bones

Scientists think this dinosaur weighed as much
as five elephants! It may be the heaviest dinosaur
ever found. This creature's neck and back bones
were light, though. Large spaces lay between
the bones, helping the dinosaur move its neck,
back, and tail.

Long-Necked Swimmers

Many dinosaurs lived in the water. This group of dinosaurs had long necks. Their long necks gave them a long, thin shape that helped them move through water. Their necks also helped them grab fish to eat.

Sea Serpent

This dinosaur's neck looks like a long snake! It did not move as well as a snake, though. The bones in this creature's neck show that it could only move from side to side. It could not move its neck up and down very well.

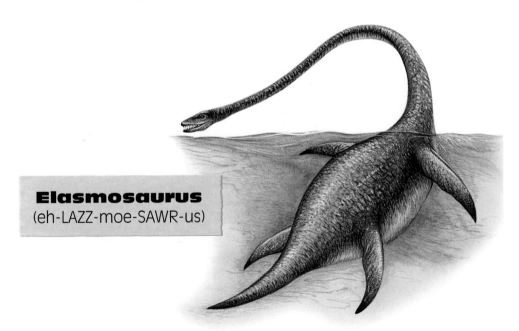

Elasmosaurus
(eh-LAZZ-moe-SAWR-us)

A Neck for Fishing

This dinosaur's neck had seventy-one bones. Its neck was more than half the length of its body! This creature could stick its neck into a school of fish. Then it grabbed the fish in its mouth.

Elasmosaur
(eh-LAZZ-moe-SAWR)

Arambourgiania
(a-rahm-BOOR-jee-AN-ee-a)

Long-Necked Flyer

Some prehistoric creatures could fly. This flying reptile's wings stretched wider than three cars laid end to end.

Scientists had trouble identifying the parts of this creature's fossil. They first thought the many neck bones held up the wings. They later figured out that the creature had a really long neck!

Compsognathus
(COMP-sag-NAY-thus)

Small Dinosaur, Long Neck

Not all dinosaurs were big. This dinosaur was only
about the size of a chicken. Its body was small, but
its tail and neck were long! It reached out its long
neck to grab its prey.

Heavy Necks

Not all dinosaur necks were long and thin. This dinosaur had a thick, heavy neck. It had to be big to hold up the dinosaur's huge head. The neck also had big muscles. They helped the dinosaur open and close its powerful jaws. A dinosaur's neck helped it in many ways.

Allosaurus
(AL-oh-SAWR-us)

Glossary

arc — a curved line

armor —scales or spikes that cover some animals and help protect them

fossils — remains of an animal or plant that lived millions of years ago

identifying — telling what something is

muscles — parts of the body that pull on the bones to make them move

predators — animals that hunt other animals for food

prey — an animal that is hunted for food

skeleton — the bones that support and protect the body

snouts — long noses that stick out at the front of some animals' heads

weapons —things that can be used in a fight

For More Information

Books

Dinosaurs! The Biggest Baddest Strangest Fastest.
Howard Zimmerman (Atheneum)

I Wonder Why Triceratops Had Horns and Other Questions About Dinosaurs. Rod Theodorou (Kingfisher)

Seismosaurus (Heinemann First Library). Rupert Matthews (Heinemann Library)

Stegosaurus and Other Plains Dinosaurs. Dougal Dixon (Picture Window Books)

Web Sites

All About Dinosaurs: Triceratops
www.enchantedlearning.com/subjects/dinosaurs/dinos/ Triceratops.shtml
Diagram, facts about this dinosaur's diet and behavior, plus a picture to print out and color

Dinosaur National Monument
www.cr.nps.gov/museum/exhibits/dino/adaptation.html
How fossils help scientists figure out dinosaur necks and spikes

Index

armor 7

back 4, 6, 7, 8, 15
bones 13, 15, 17, 18
dog 8
elephants 10, 15
eyes 10
fighting 4
fish 16, 18
flying 19
food 11
fossils 19
head 5, 7, 9, 11, 21
horns 5

jaws 21
nose 5
plates 6
predators 4, 7
prey 20
shoulders 7, 8
snouts 9, 10
tails 6, 7, 8, 14, 15, 20
trees 11, 12
Triceratops 10
weapons 9

About the Author

Joanne Mattern is the author of more than 130 books for children. Her favorite subjects are animals, history, sports, and biographies. Joanne lives in New York State with her husband, three young daughters, and three crazy cats.